MW00948381

WHAT ARE MONDAYS GOOD FOR, ANYWAY?

Written by Nicole Frankel

Illustrated by Annette Wood

© 2023 Nicole Frankel

Published by Nicole Frankel Books
555 Madison Avenue, 5th Floor
New York, NY 10022

www.nicolefrankelbooks.com
nicole@nicolefrankelbooks.com

Illustration by Annette Wood: www.AnnetteWoodGraphics.com

ISBN: 979-8-9876043-1-1

Printed in the United States.

To Eleanor, Brooks, and Everett,

Mama loves you all the way
to Neptune's storms and back.

Bennie hates **MONDAYS.**

Mondays mean: No more chocolate chip pancakes covered in ooey-gooey syrup...

Hmmm...
a brand-new
box of
Marshmallow
Crunchies—
his favorite
breakfast.

Could this **MONDAY** be different?

MARSHMALLOW
CRUNCHIES

Bennie excitedly poured the yummy cereal into his bowl. But instead of a rainbow of marshmallows...two stinky green socks tumbled out of the box!

Bennie scowled.

"LENNIE! DID YOU PUT YOUR DIRTY SOCKS IN THE CEREAL BOX?!"

But as Bennie stared at the socks in his cereal bowl, he realized that he didn't feel mad. In fact, his scowl turned into a little smile.

MONDAYS
aren't for smiles,
but oh, what a sight,
and some things in life
make your heart light.

MARSHMALLOW CRUNCHIES

Bennie grabbed a handful of Wheatballs—the icky cereal—and headed to the bus stop while thinking of all the things waiting for him at school today:

a spelling test, "mystery" meatloaf for lunch,
and recess inside the boring classroom.

Next thing he knew, he was tumbling toward the ground.

"UGH!

This could only happen on a

MONDAY!"

At that moment, Bennie noticed something staring up at him from the puddle. The Wheatballs had landed in the shape of a smiley face!

Again, Bennie felt something odd inside as his mouth curled into a wide grin.

MONDAYS

aren't for grins, but oh, what a sight,
and some things in life make your heart light.

Bennie arrived at school with butterflies in his stomach. SPELLING TESTS are as bad as a METEOR heading to Earth!

He closed his eyes and tried to practice some of his spelling words in his head.

When Bennie opened his eyes, he noticed three pencils dangling from the ceiling over his teacher's head.

Then it happened...

One by one, the pencils fell right into Miss Kitty's hair. Miss Kitty looked like a porcupine, but she just kept on teaching.

Bennie began to laugh, quietly at first and then so loudly that even Miss Kitty heard.

MONDAYS aren't for laughs, but oh, what a sight, and some things in life make your heart light.

Lunchtime arrived.

The cafeteria lady, Miss Clemmie, made a mean corndog and the best cheese pizza around— but not on **MONDAYS**, of course.

And because mystery meatloaf wasn't bad enough, she always served it with green Jell-O that looked like oozy Galaxy Slime.

Bennie picked up the Jell-O to inspect it and gave it a good squeeze.

The green sludge
shot out of the cup
and landed with a
SPLAT!
on the cafeteria wall.

TALENT
SHOW
TRYOUTS

Oh, Miss Clemmie was going to be so mad. But Bennie felt that odd thing again. He laughed. And this time, he couldn't stop. He laughed until tears sprang from his eyes.

MONDAYS
aren't for happy
tears, but oh, what
a sight, and some
things in life make
your heart light.

TALENT
SHOW
TRYOUTS

Bennie's dad picked him up from school and told him he was taking him to his favorite park.

But then came the sign with the dreadful words…

PARK CLOSED

"Doesn't it just figure that the park would be closed on a **MONDAY!**"

PARK CLOSED

WHOOSH!

A strong gust of wind blew the sign off the gate.

PARK CLOSED

It swirled through the air and landed with a SMACK! on the BEHIND of a big yellow dog!

No one seemed to notice.

But Bennie certainly *did*, and it was the funniest thing he'd ever seen.

Bennie laughed and laughed and laughed until he was laughing so hard that he was rolling around in the grass with the big yellow dog.

He tried his best to stop—it was

MONDAY

after all—but oh, what a sight, and some things in life make your heart light.

At dinnertime, everyone in Bennie's family took turns talking about their day. When it was Bennie's turn, he told of his stinky breakfast, the grinning puddle, Miss Kitty's porcupine hair, the green Jell-O on the wall, and the sign on the dog's behind.

As he described his day, Bennie realized something. It wasn't odd at all to laugh on a Monday. It felt like the most normal thing on the planet.

First, he cracked a little smile.

Then, that little smile turned into a full grin.

Bennie began to laugh until he was laughing so hard that tears rolled down his cheeks.

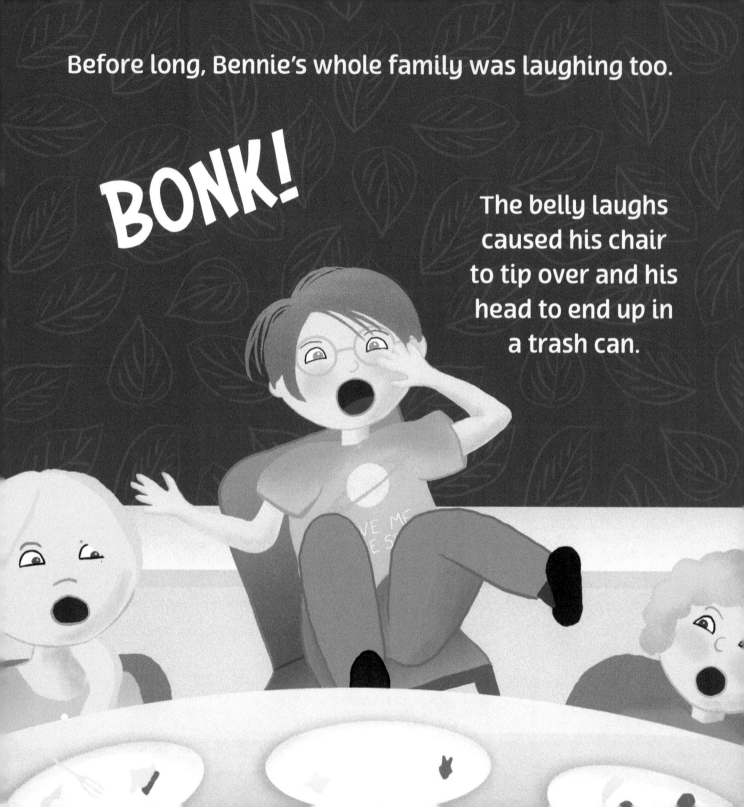

Bennie removed the trash can, and the laughter stopped—but not for long. Bennie, with his trash-covered head, was the funniest thing his family had ever seen!

Bennie joined in, and
when the laughing
spell was over, he said,

"Now I know what

MONDAYS

are good for:

LAUGHS!"

Printed in the USA
CPSIA information can be obtained
at www.ICGtesting.com
LVHW070748151023
761120LV00015B/769